W9-CII-148

Another Sommer-Time Story

The
Great
Royal Race

By Carl Sommer
Illustrated by Dick Westbrook

Advance • HOUSTON
PUBLISHING, INC

Permissions
Advance Publishing, Inc.
6950 Fulton St.
Houston, TX 77022

http://www.advancepublishing.com

First Edition
Printed in Singapore

Library of Congress Cataloging-in-Publication Data

Sommer, Carl, 1930-
    The great royal race / by Carl Sommer ; illustrated by Dick
Westbrook. – 1st ed.
        p. cm. – (Another Sommer-time story)
    Summary: With the help of her father a princess designs a race
among three suitors for her hand in marriage that will reveal her
one true love.
    ISBN 1-57537-008-5 (hc : alk. paper). – ISBN 1-57537-054-9 (lib.
bdg. : alk. paper)
    [1. Princesses–Fiction. 2. Kings, queens, rulers, etc.–Fiction.
3. Running–Fiction.] I. Westbrook, Dick, ill. II. Title.
III. Series: Sommer, Carl, 1930- Another Sommer-time story.
PZ7.S696235Gr 1997
[E]–dc20   96-24346
                                                                 CIP
                                                                  AC

The Great Royal Race

Once upon a time, in a land far away, there lived a lovely young princess named Elizabeth.

She was kind and gracious, the delight of the kingdom. And now that she had come of age, it was time for her to choose ... her one true love.

From across the land came three fine suitors—Simon, Thomas, and John.

Simon was trained in the finest of schools and was charming to all the fair maidens. He knew what to say and just how to say it, and he knew how to get what he wanted. Simon wanted to be a wealthy prince!

Thomas was strong and handsome—a captain in the Royal Guard. When he rode into town dressed in his shining armor, the young women adored him. But Thomas had lofty dreams. He planned to marry the princess, for she was in line to the throne. And the royal decree stated that whomever she married would be the next king.

"I'll ride a white horse and parade through the towns," he boasted. "All the people will rush from their homes just to catch a glimpse of...ME!"

And then there was John—a commoner and a dreamer.

The day he and the princess first met, John was covered with mud. He was helping an old man get his wagon out of a ditch.

"Who is that man?" asked the princess.

Those nearby answered, "His name is John. He is a good man—always helping someone."

Elizabeth walked over to John. "'It's a fine thing you're doing—lending a helping hand."

"Thank you," said John, wiping his face. He then looked up at the kindhearted princess and suddenly fell deeply in love.

When John told his friends, they laughed at him. "Forget it! You weren't born to be a prince."

"Maybe she will become a commoner," he said.

"It's utterly hopeless," his friends told him.

But by the time the princess had gotten back to the castle, something strange had happened to her—she could not get John out of her mind.

From early on Elizabeth's mother had taught her, "You are a wealthy princess, and many men will want to marry you. Be careful, and choose your prince wisely."

The queen would explain, "Seek a man of good character—one who will honor and respect you. Such a man will never ask you to do anything wrong.

"You must find the one who truly loves you. Then it will not matter to him whether you are rich or poor, sick or well, a princess or a peasant."

Each of the suitors had always behaved with honor—at least around the princess.

Still she wondered, "If I choose a prince, how can I be certain he really loves me? Perhaps he wants only to be rich and famous."

At last she decided, "I'll ask Father. He'll know what to do!"

Down the hall and past the guards went the beautiful princess.

"Father, may I speak with you?"

With a snap of his finger, the king cleared the room.

Elizabeth then told her father about Simon, Thomas, and John. She asked him how she could be sure to choose the right prince.

The king sat quietly thinking.

"I have an idea!" the king finally said. He shared with her what he thought she should do.

"Excellent!" said Elizabeth. "That will show who really loves me."

Elizabeth thanked her father and left the palace excited about what was going to happen.

Elizabeth called her three suitors to the courtyard and told them about the test.

"His Majesty, the king, has planned a race. It is a test of true love. The winner of the Great Royal Race...shall be my prince."

When Elizabeth left, the three men talked about the race.

"If I win," exclaimed Simon, raising his hands, "I'll become a wealthy prince!"

"If I win," boasted Thomas, "I'll be famous!" He stuck out his chest and bellowed, "For *I...* will be the next king!"

John simply whispered, "If I win, I'll marry the most lovely and kind person in the world."

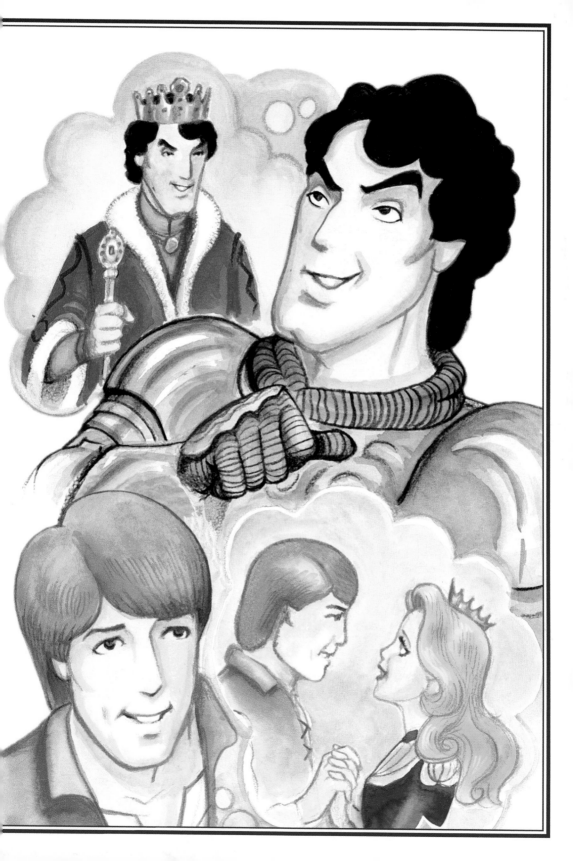

Back at the palace, the princess chatted with her ladies-in-waiting. The race would be such an exciting time for all. Elizabeth's heart was already pounding—for soon she would discover her one true love.

Day after day Simon, Thomas, and John trained hard for the race. Whether pouring rain or searing heat, the suitors ran...and ran... and ran. They knew the chance to marry the princess was worth every sacrifice.

The Great Royal Race was the talk of the kingdom. No one had ever heard of such an event.

Some even complained, "The princess is very foolish for having a race to decide on a prince!"

Meanwhile, the king called three of his most trusted servants. He told them, "This race is very, very important."

After explaining the plan, the king gave each of his servants a brown leather bag...and one final warning, "Don't let anyone see you!"

"Yes, Your Majesty," came the answer. "Be assured no one will find out."

Finally it arrived—the day of the Great Royal Race. People from all the towns and villages of the kingdom lined the streets. Everyone, both young and old, had come to see the race.

The king, queen, and princess took their places in the Royal Grandstand.

With great joy the runners approached the starting line. Their hearts beat with excitement.

Each one had trained long and hard for this moment. Finally they would discover who would have the honor of marrying the beautiful princess.

"Who do you think will win?" whispered a woman.

"It will definitely be either Thomas or Simon," a man quickly answered. "Both are much faster than John."

This was true, and John knew it. Still he purposed in his heart, "I may not be the fastest, but I'm going to try as hard as I can."

The crowds cheered as the suitors walked to the starting line.

The king read the rules. Then with a loud voice he announced, "When the town bell rings, the race begins!"

A hush fell over the crowd.

"Clang! Clang!" went the town bell, and like a flash of lightning, Simon, Thomas, and John dashed from the starting line.

The crowds cheered! The Great Royal Race was under way!

Further up the path, the king's servants heard the bells and all the cheering. They knew the race had begun—and they also had prepared for this day. Hiding along the way, they were ready to obey the king's command.

Around the first bend came Simon and Thomas, with John slightly behind. When the servant spotted the runners, he tossed three gold coins onto the path.

"W-w-wow!" cried Simon and Thomas, spotting the valuable coins. Their hearts beat with excitement as they quickly picked up the gold.

But not John. He did not miss a step. His heart was fixed on the kind-hearted princess.

Of course, Simon and Thomas also wanted to marry the princess, but how could they possibly pass up this great treasure? Besides, they knew they could easily outrun John.

Simon and Thomas quickly made up for lost time. But as they rounded the second corner, they could hardly believe their eyes.

"More gold!" yelled Thomas.

He and Simon dashed for the riches—but John kept running.

It was not long until Simon and Thomas passed John again. As they came to the final turn, the runners caught a glimpse of three more pieces of gold—and these were much larger than the others!

"I'm rich! I'm rich!" cried Simon.

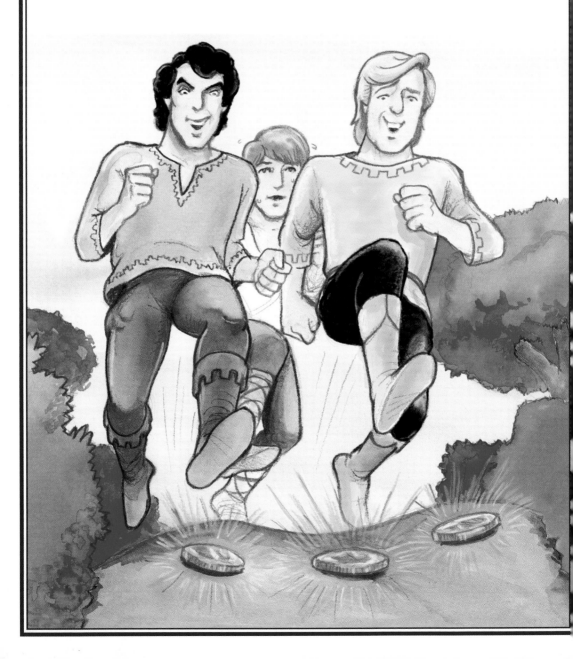

The greedy pair dove for the gold. But John never even looked at it—he just kept running.

Simon grabbed one coin, Thomas snatched another. For the last piece of gold, the two men wrestled.

"Give it to me!" Thomas shouted. "I saw it first."

"No!" yelled Simon. "It's mine!"

They fought over the coin until Thomas finally said, "I'll let you carry it. But I warn you, we're going to settle this later!"

"You bet we will!" snapped Simon.

Quickly the pair dusted themselves. They did not want anyone to know they had stopped for the gold—especially the princess.

Then off they went—running as fast as they could, all the while grinning at the sound of gold jingling in their pockets.

As the runners came into view, the beautiful princess stood up, cheering them on to the finish.

Although Simon and Thomas were gaining ground, they began wondering if perhaps they were foolish for having stopped for the gold.

"I must try harder," Simon huffed, "if I am to be a wealthy prince." He picked up speed.

Thomas ran faster than ever. "I must...I must win," he cried, "or I'll never become a famous king!"

Only his love for Elizabeth pushed John along. "I'll do whatever it takes to win the princess." He strained every muscle in his body to run faster. But would it be enough?

At the very last second, all three runners gave a final burst of speed.

The crowd cheered as the runners crossed the finish line. The race was over—the commoner had won!

Simon and Thomas were very angry. They had come so close, yet they had lost the race.

Elizabeth was delighted. Now she knew who really loved her...and not just her wealth and fame.

With tears in her eyes she went to John and said, "You are my prince."

John gave a big smile and said, "And you are my princess!"

The princess then went to her father and kissed him. She thanked him for helping her find her one and only true love.

Now all the people in the kingdom praised the king for his great wisdom in testing the suitors with gold.

However, throughout the towns and villages, Simon and Thomas became known as the "Foolish Ones."

Soon afterward the kingdom rejoiced as the wedding bells chimed, announcing the marriage of John and Elizabeth.

The king and queen provided a grand marriage feast. Everyone was invited to join in the celebration.

Elizabeth was forever grateful for her father's wise advise. Not only did John prove that he truly loved her, but in time he also proved that he was born to rule.

John became a very wise and great king, and he and Elizabeth lived happily ever after.